BASED ON THE BOOK BY BRAM STOKER

DRACULA

BASED ON THE BOOK BY BRAM STOKER

Retold by
Mary Sebag-Montefiore

Reading consultant: Alison Kelly

Edited by Jane Chisholm and Rachel Firth

Designed by Matthew Preston

Cover illustrations by Ryan Quickfall

Inside illustrations by Ian McNee

First published in 2019 by Usborne Publishing Ltd., Usborne House,
83-85 Saffron Hill, London EC1N 8RT, England.
www.usborne.com

Contents

Chapter 1
Journey Into Darkness

Jonathan Harker's Journal

May 3

Arrived in Buda-Pesht, a wonderful place. Delicious dinner in my hotel: chicken done with red pepper and paprika. (Memo: get recipe for Mina.) I slept badly – there was a dog howling outside my window, but woke in good time to catch my next train to Bistritz, into the very heart of Transylvania.

Count Dracula had instructed me to spend this night at the Golden Krone Hotel, and then travel by coach next day to the Borgo Pass, where his own carriage would be waiting to drive me to his castle.

May 4

I had a strange encounter with the landlady of the hotel. When I told her where I was going, she made the sign of the cross and refused to speak further. Then, just before I left, she cried, "Must you go, young Herr?"

I have important business there," I replied.

"Do you know what you are going to?" she implored, falling onto her knees. Then she offered me her crucifix. I had always considered such things idolatrous or superstitious, but I felt it rude to refuse such a kindly-intended gift. She put it around my neck, saying, "For your mother's sake."

I am wearing it now, as I write my journal.

A crowd had gathered round me as I boarded the coach, all crossing themselves, all looking kind but pitying me. Not very pleasant for me, setting off to an unknown place to meet an unknown man. But I soon forgot my fears in the beauty of the scenes we passed through: a mass of fruit blossoms, apple, plum, pear, cherry; the grassy curves of fields spangled with petals. The land swelled into hills and then into the lofty sweeps of the Carpathian Mountains, an endless succession of jagged rocks and pointed crags. The deep blues and purples in the afternoon sun were glorious in the shadows of the peaks.

When it grew dark, the other passengers seemed to grow anxious, urging our driver on. We had entered the Borgo Pass. Our horses began to snort and plunge wildly. We had been overtaken by a carriage with four black horses, driven by a man with a long brown beard and a hat which hid his face. I could only see the gleam of his bright eyes which seemed red in the lamplight.

"My passenger," he said, pointing to me. "Give me his luggage."

As he spoke, he smiled, and I could see his mouth was hard, with very red lips and sharp teeth, white as ivory.

I climbed into his carriage and we sped away into the night. I could just hear the words of another passenger calling his farewell to me, quoting a line of a poem:

For the dead travel fast.

Then a dog began to wail, as if in fear. The sound was taken up by another dog, then another till, borne upon the wind which sighed softly through the Pass, came another sound, a wild howling, growing louder and sharper. Wolves!

The wind moaned and whistled through the rock, and branches of the trees crashed together as we passed. Snow began to fall. The driver seemed undisturbed, even when the moon, sailing through the black clouds, appeared behind a jagged crag, and in its light I saw a ring of wolves. White teeth they had, and lolling tongues, and long, sinewy limbs.

I saw the driver in the roadway, sweeping his long arms, his voice raised in a tone of imperious command. The wolves fell back, and back further still. As he climbed up again into the carriage, I saw the wolves had disappeared. So strange and uncanny was this that a dreadful fear swept over me. Just then a cloud blotted out the moon so that we were again in darkness.

We kept on climbing up the steep, twisting road, till at last I became aware that the driver was pulling into the courtyard of a vast ruined castle. From its tall windows came no ray of light and its broken battlements showed up as a jagged line against the ghostly sky.

The driver jumped down and helped me out. His fingers felt like a steel trap that could have crushed me if he had chosen. He took my luggage, jumped back into the carriage, shook up the horses, and disappeared into the night.

I was by a great, old door, studded with nails. There was no bell or knocker. I didn't know what to do. No one would have been able to hear me call through that door.

What sort of place had I come to?

This was not the usual sort of destination for a

lawyer like me, sent to explain the purchase of a London house to a foreigner. I felt I was in a nightmare and must wait patiently in its clutches until morning came. Just as I was thinking this, the door opened to the sound of rattling chains and the clanking of massive bolts being drawn back. In the gleam of an antique silver lamp stood a tall old man, dressed from head to toe in black. He gestured me in, saying in excellent English, but with strange intonation:

"Welcome. Enter freely and of your own will!"

The moment I crossed his threshold, he seized my hand with a strength that made me wince, very like the handshake I had noticed in the driver. I had not seen that man's face, so to make sure it was not the same person, I said:

"Count Dracula?"

"I am Dracula. Come in, the night is chill, and you need to eat and rest. It is late, and my servants are not available, so I must see to your comfort myself."

I followed him up a great winding staircase and down a stone passage on which our footsteps rang loudly. At the end of it he threw open a heavy door, and I rejoiced to see a table spread for supper and a mighty hearth with flaming logs. The Count opened another door to a small octagonal room with no window. Passing through this, he opened yet another door into a bedroom, with, I was glad to see, a blazing fire that went up the chimney with a hollow roar. All my doubts and fears vanished in the warmth, and I discovered I was famished.

"I pray you, be seated," said the Count as we returned to the first room. "I will not dine with you because I have already eaten." He took the covers off the dishes to reveal an excellent roast chicken, some cheese and a salad. This, with an excellent bottle of old Tokay – of which I had two glasses – was my supper.

While I ate and drank, the Count asked me about my journey. I was able to observe him as we spoke. His face was strong and eagle-like. His eyebrows were massive, and his mouth was rather cruel-looking, with peculiarly sharp white teeth that hung over his lips, that were astonishingly red and youthful for a man of his age.

His hands were broad, with squat fingers, and oddly, there were hairs on the middle of his palms. His nails were long and cut to a sharp point. As he leaned over to pour my wine, I smelled his foul breath.

Dawn was now breaking. I heard a chorus of wolves howling.

"Listen to the music of the children of the night," said the Count, his eyes gleaming. "Tomorrow, I must be absent for a while, but you will find breakfast in the dining room. I trust you will stay here for some time, so I can improve my English. I love England. Tell me about the property which my friend, your senior partner, Peter Hawkins, has found for me."

"It is just outside London. It is called Carfax, a very large, dilapidated house in twenty acres, with a high wall around it, and heavy gates. Parts of it are very old – one part has very thick walls and just a few windows high up, barred with iron. It looks like part of a medieval castle, and is close to an old chapel. There are many trees and there's a pond... some might find it gloomy. There are no houses nearby."

"I love shade and shadow. I am glad it is big, and rejoice at the chapel. We Transylvanian nobles cannot lay our bones among the common dead."

MAY 5

He left me then. I was not sleepy, but I went to bed feeling uneasy. There was something strange about this place.

When I rose in the morning, I hung my own shaving mirror on the wall and began to shave. There was no other mirror in the room. Suddenly I felt a hand on my shoulder, and heard the Count say, "Good morning."

I jumped. There he was behind me, yet he was invisible in the glass. I saw I had cut myself slightly and the blood was trickling a little down my chin. When I turned to look for some sticking plaster, the Count grabbed my throat, with a blaze of demonic fury in his eyes. I pulled away, and his hand touched my crucifix.

Instantly, his anger vanished.

"Take care," he said. "It is more dangerous than you think to cut yourself in this country." Then, seizing my shaving mirror, he opened the window with a wrench and flung it outside, where it shattered into a thousand pieces on the courtyard far below. Then he left. It is very annoying, as I do not see how I can shave without a mirror.

I went downstairs to the dining room, where breakfast was laid out. There was no sign of the Count. I realized I had never seen him eat or drink. At breakfast, I saw from the window that the castle was on the edge of a giant precipice. As far as the eye can see is a canopy of green treetops, with the occasional rift where there is a deep gorge and rivers wind through the depths. I tried to explore further into the castle after breakfast. There were doors, doors everywhere, and all of them were locked. In no place, apart from the view from the windows, was there any means of escape.

This castle is a prison! I am a prisoner here.

A wild feeling came over me, and I rushed to the doors again, trying each one without success, and peering out of the windows. I behaved like a rat in a trap… I think I must have gone mad for a time. Then I sat down to think it over quietly. No good talking to the Count. He knew as well as I that I was a prisoner; it was by his own hand.

I went cautiously to my bedroom, and found the Count making my bed. This confirmed my suspicions. There were no servants. He and I were alone. With a fright, I realized that he must have been the coachman. That meant he could control wolves, just by raising his hand. Thank heavens for the crucifix. Whenever I touched it, it gave me strength.

CHAPTER 2
SECRETS OF CASTLE DRACULA

JONATHAN HARKER'S JOURNAL CONTINUED

That night we talked of legal matters concerning the house he wished to buy. He told me to write to my senior partner, Mr. Hawkins, informing him that I would be here for some time. Seeing my horrified look, he added angrily: "I understood that my needs only were to be considered."

I bowed assent. What else could I do? I had no choice.

"Write only about business in your letter," said the Count. "You may tell your friends that you are well, and had a good journey." With a smile that showed his sharp teeth, he handed me three sheets of paper and three envelopes. I understood I was to be careful, for he would read my letters.

I wrote to Mr. Hawkins, enclosing another letter to Mina, in my secret shorthand code.

The count took my envelope and stamped it.

"I must leave you now," he said. "Let me warn you. Go where you wish where the doors are open, but beware! Only fall asleep in your own room. The castle is old, and has many memories which make bad dreams for those who sleep unwisely."

Another warning. I wondered: could any dream be as terrible as the net of mystery which seemed to be closing around me?

LATER

When he left me, I went up the stone stairs that led to my room, and looked out of the window. There was some relief in the vast view, bathed in the soft yellow moonlight. As I leaned out, I saw a movement below me, from where I knew the Count's own rooms were.

What I saw was the Count's head, then his entire body emerging. My feelings turned to terror, for he began to crawl down the castle wall, face down, his cloak spreading about him. I saw his fingers and toes grasp the corners of the stones, as he moved speedily, like a lizard.

What sort of man is this? I am in fear. I feel the dread of this horrible place overpowering me.

Now he was absent, I decided to explore the castle. I took a lamp and down to the great hall, but the doors around it were locked. The key, I thought, must be in the Count's room. I climbed the stone staircase. One or two rooms I found unlocked, but there was nothing in them except some dusty, worm-eaten furniture. I came to another door and tried to open it. It gave way as I pushed hard against it.

Inside, the furniture was more comfortable than any I had seen so far. Surely this room had once, long ago, seen gentle, happy lives. The moonlight poured in through the diamond-shaped window panes, and I felt a quietness steal over me, a comfort after the chill of the castle. I took out my diary and a pen from my pocket, and wrote up the events of the day. Writing always soothes me.

I began to feel sleepy. I remembered the Count's warning, but took pleasure in disobeying it. I put my diary and pen back in my pocket and fell asleep – at least, I hope so, for all that followed seemed startlingly real.

In the moonlight opposite me were three young ladies. Two were dark, and the third had great wavy masses of golden hair and eyes like sapphires. All three had brilliant white teeth and ruby red lips. They whispered together and laughed. The dark one said, "Go on, you first, and then we will follow."

The fair girl came towards me, bending as if to kiss me. I felt her hot breath on my neck, and then the dent of two sharp teeth on my flesh.

In that instant, the Count appeared in a storm of fury, the red light in his eyes lurid, as if fires blazed in them. Never did I imagine such wrath. With a fierce sweep of his arm he pulled the girl back, hurling her down, hissing: "This man belongs to me! How dare you touch him, any of you, when I have forbidden it! I promise you that when I am done with him, you shall kiss him all you want. Now go! Go! I must awaken him, for there is work to be done."

"Are we to have nothing tonight?" asked one of them with a low laugh.

In answer, he nodded his head, then threw a bag on the floor. It moved as though there were some living thing inside it. One of the women jumped forward and opened it. There was a gasp and a low wail. The women closed around while I was frozen with horror, but as I looked, they disappeared, and with them that dreadful bag. There was no door near them. They simply seemed to fade into the rays of the moonlight and pass through the window

– I could see their dim, shadowy forms outside for a moment before they entirely faded away.

Then horror overcame me, and I sank into unconsciousness.

When I woke, I was in my own room, in my bed. Was it all a dream, I wondered? No. The Count must have carried me here. There were small pieces of evidence to prove this. My clothes were on a chair, folded in a manner unlike my habits, and my watch was unwound: I always wind it before going to bed. I am glad that the Count must have been in too much of a hurry to check my pockets, for everything in them was still there – including my diary, thank goodness. My room, I felt, although it had been so full of fear to me, was now a sort of sanctuary, for nothing could be more dreadful than those women who were – who are – waiting to suck my blood.

The next morning, the Count asked me, in the calmest of tones that allowed for no contradiction, to write three letters: one saying my work was nearly done, another to say I was starting for home, and the third that I had left the castle and arrived at Bistritz. I obeyed. It would be madness to quarrel with him when I am so totally in his power. To refuse would arouse his anger and excite his suspicion. I asked him the dates I should put on my letters.

He calculated a moment, then said:

"The first should be June 12, the second June 19, the third, June 29."

I now know the span of my life, God help me.

MAY 23

There is a chance of escape. A band of gypsies are camping around the castle. I have written to Mr. Hawkins, asking him to communicate with Mina. To her, I have written in shorthand code, not telling her everything, as I don't want to alarm her. I sealed the letters and threw them from my window to the gypsy men below, with some coins, making what signs I could to have them posted. The man who took them pressed them to his heart, and bowed, then put them in his cap. I could do no more. I went into my room, and began to read.

…All hope of my correspondence being sent is lost. The Count has just come in. In his smoothest voice he said, "The gypsies have given me two letters, one to our friend, Mr. Hawkins, which I shall take care of. Unfortunately, the seal has broken. Your letters are of course precious to me. Will you address it again?"

He handed me a fresh envelope. I could only redirect it, and hand it to him in silence.

"The other letter…" He pulled it out of its envelope as he spoke, displaying the strange symbols of my shorthand, "is a vile thing, an outrage to friendship and hospitality. Well! It cannot matter to us. I shall burn it."

He flung it in the fire, his eyes blazing wickedly, as letter and envelope were reduced to ashes.

He left the room and I heard the key turn softly. A minute later I went over and tried it. The door was locked.

After an hour or two, the Count came in again. He was very polite and cheery in his manner, saying, "So, my friend, are you tired? Get to bed. I will not have the pleasure of talking to you tonight, as there is much work I have to do, but I hope you will sleep well."

Strange to say, I slept without dreaming. Despair has its own calms.

MAY 24

This morning, when I woke, I decided to get some writing paper and envelopes out of my bag, and keep them in my pocket, so I could write again if I should get the opportunity. But again a surprise, again a shock!

Every scrap of paper had gone – taken by an unseen hand, including my notes on train times, my letters of credit enabling me to draw money. Everything in fact, that might be useful to me if I could get outside the castle.

Driven by dark thoughts, I looked in the wardrobe, and then went over to my suitcase.

All my clothes had gone – my suit, my overcoat and my travel rug. I could find no trace of them anywhere.

May 25

This morning, as I was sitting on my bed, racking my brains, I heard through the window a cracking of whips and scraping of horses' hooves.

It was the gypsies, their wagons drawn by eight sturdy horses, their drivers wearing wide hats, nail-studded belts, dirty sheepskin and high boots. I ran to the door, intending to go downstairs and join them, but it was locked.

I ran to the window and cried out to them. They looked up at me stupidly and pointed, but just then the head man came out, and seeing them pointing, said something at which they laughed. After that, no effort of mine, no piteous, loud cry would make them even look at me. They turned away, and drove off.

Shortly after, I heard the cracking of their whips die away in the distance.

May 26

I was looking out of my window before morning when I saw something emerging from the Count's window. I drew back and watched carefully. It was the Count. It was a new shock to me to see he was wearing my suit. Slung over his shoulder was the terrible bag which I had seen the three women take away. There could be no doubt of his purpose – and in my own clothes too! This, then, is his new scheme of evil. He will make others think they have seen me, alive and well, in the towns and villages, and any wickedness he may do to the local people shall be attributed to me. It made me rage to think this could go on, while I am shut up here a prisoner, but without the protection of the law, which is every prisoner's right.

I thought I would watch for the Count's return, and for a long time sat at the window. Hours passed till moonlight fell. Then I began to notice little specks floating in its rays. They were like the tiniest specks of dust, and they whirled around gathering into clusters. I watched them, finding this strange phantasm almost soothing, and I leaned back comfortably, so I could enjoy more fully this dance of dust.

Something made me start up... the low howling of dogs far below in the valley, hidden from my sight. Louder it rang in my ears, and the floating motes of dust began to take new shapes as they moved in rhythm with the sounds. I felt hypnotized as I watched, though I struggled against letting my sensibilities flow with the dance. Quicker and quicker danced the dust, and the moonbeams seemed to quiver as they lit the mass of darkness beyond. More and more the motes gathered, till they began to take shape. And then I was jerked into stark consciousness, fully awake, and screamed. The phantom shapes which were gradually becoming materialized from the moonlight were those of the three ghastly women to whom I was doomed. I screamed again, and lit my lamp, to block out the moonlight.

After a couple of hours I heard a sound coming from the Count's room – something like a sharp wail, quickly cut off. I tried my door, but I was locked in my prison. I could do nothing.

I sat down and cried.

As I sat, I heard a stirring in the courtyard below – the agonized cry of a woman. I rushed to the window, and, throwing it open, peered out. There, below, was a woman with unkempt hair, holding her hands over her heart, as if out of breath with running. When she saw my face at the window, she threw herself forward, crying, "Monster! Give me my child!"

She flung herself on her knees, raising up her hands, and cried again the same words, in tones that wrung my heart. Then she tore her hair, and threw herself at the door. I could hear her beating it with her fists.

High overhead, probably on the tower, I heard the voice of the Count, calling in his harsh whisper. His call seemed to be answered from far and wide by the howling of wolves. Before many minutes had passed, a pack of them poured into the courtyard, like a pent-up dam liberated, its water flowing fast and furious.

The woman's cries suddenly stopped and the howling of the wolves ended abruptly. Soon they streamed away, licking their lips.

I could not be sorry. I knew now what had happened to the child, and perhaps the mother was better dead.

What shall I do? What can I do? How shall I escape from this dreadful destiny of night and dark and fear?

Chapter 3

From Fear To Courage

June 25

No man knows till he has suffered from the night, how sweet to the heart and eye is the morning.

When the sun rose in the sky, my fear fell from me as if it had dissolved in the warmth. I must take some sort of action, while the courage of the day is upon me.

Last night the first of my post-dated letters was sent; the first of the three which are to blot out the traces of my existence.

Let me not think of it. Action!

It struck me that it is always at night that I have been threatened or have been in some way in danger or in fear. I have never seen the Count in daylight. Can it be that he sleeps when others are awake, so that he is awake while others sleep? If only I could get into his room. But his door is always locked. I need to find the key to the outer door, and with it, my chance of escape.

Yes, there is a way, if one dares to take it. I have seen him crawl from his window. Why shouldn't I imitate him, and go in by his window? The chances are desperate, but I am desperate too. I shall risk it. At worst, it can only result in death.

Goodbye, Mina, if I fail. God help me in my task.

SAME DAY, LATER

I did it! And I am back safely in my own room. I went while my courage was still fresh. I climbed out of the window, onto the narrow ledge which runs outside. The stones were roughly cut, and the mortar between them had over time been worn away. I took my boots off, and looked down once, to make sure that a sudden glance of that awful depth would not overcome me. After that, I kept my eyes from it. I knew where the Count's window was, and made for it. I was too excited to feel dizzy. Eventually, I reached his windowsill, raised up the sash and I slid inside. Looking around for the Count, I was glad to find the room was empty.

It was barely furnished. Such furniture as there was seemed to have never been used. The only thing of interest was a heap of gold in one corner – gold of all kinds, Roman and British and Austrian, and Hungarian and Greek and Turkish money, all covered with a film of dust as though it had long laid there. None, I noticed, was less than three hundred years old. There were also chains and ornaments and jewels, all old and stained.

No key, anywhere. I had to search further.

In another corner was a heavy door. It was open, and led through a stone passage to a circular stairway, which went steeply down. I followed it, going carefully, for the only light came from holes in the mortar surrounding the heavy stones. At the bottom was a dark tunnel-like passage, and wafting out of it was a deathly, sickly smell of old earth, freshly dug. As I went down the passage, the smell grew closer and heavier. At last I pulled open another door and found myself in a ruined chapel, with a floor made of earth, which had evidently been used as a graveyard. The roof was broken. There were steps leading down into vaults, but the earth had been freshly dug over and placed in great wooden boxes. I counted them. There were fifty.

There was nobody about. I went over every inch, searching for a possible hiding place for the key. My eyes grew accustomed to the light. Down I went into the very vaults where the dim light struggled, although to do so was a dread to my heart and soul. I went into two vaults, but saw nothing there except fragments of old coffins and piles of dust. In the third, however, I made a discovery.

There, in one of the boxes lay the Count, on a pile of newly-dug earth. I could hardly tell if he were dead, or alive and asleep. His eyes were open and stony, but without the glassiness of death, and his cheeks had warmth despite their pallor. His lips were as red as ever, but there was no sign of life, no pulse, no breath, no beating of the heart. He could not have been there long, for the earthy smell would have passed away in a few hours.

I thought he might have the keys on him, and went to search, but then I saw the dead eyes. Dead though they were, they still radiated such a look of hate that I fled from the place. I left the Count's room by the window, and crawled up the castle wall.

When I reached my own room again, I threw myself, panting, on the bed, and tried to think…

JUNE 29

This evening, the date of my last letter home, the Count announced, "Tomorrow we must part. You will return to your beautiful England, and I to my work. We may never meet again. Your letter home has been sent. I shall not be here tomorrow, but all shall be ready for your journey. My carriage will come and take you to the Borgo Pass, where the stagecoach will take you to Bistritz. But I am in hopes that perhaps one day I may see you again at Castle Dracula."

I suspected him, and was determined to test his sincerity. Sincerity! What a word to use in connection with such a monster. I asked him point blank, "Why may I not leave tonight?"

"Because my coachman and horses are away on a mission."

"But I would walk with pleasure. I want to get away at once."

"And your luggage?"

"I do not care about it."

He smiled such courtesy that I rubbed my eyes.

"Not an hour shall you wait in my house against your will, though I am sad at your going, and that you so suddenly desire it. Come."

With stately gravity, he carried the lamp and led me into the great hall. Suddenly he stopped.

"Listen!" he said.

Close by, I heard the howling of wolves, almost as if the sound had sprung from his hand, as a conductor elicits sound from an orchestra. He paused a moment, then opened the door, drawing back the heavy bolts and unhooking the chains. To my astonishment, there was no key, and it was unlocked.

As the door began to open, the howling of the wolves grew louder and angrier. In they came, leaping through the door, actually inside the castle, with their red jaws, their champing teeth and clawed feet. I knew that to struggle against the Count at that moment was useless. With allies such as these at his command, I could do nothing.

Still the door continued slowly to open, and only the Count's body stood in the gap. It struck me that I was to be given to the wolves. This might be the moment and the means of my doom. There was just the sort of diabolical wickedness in the idea – the disregard for human life – that the Count might like. As a last chance, I cried out, "Shut the door. I will wait till morning." I covered my face with my hands to hide my tears of bitter disappointment.

With one sweep of his powerful arm, the Count made to throw the door shut. The wolves slunk out, and the great bolts clanged and echoed through the hall as they shot back into the night.

In silence, we left the hall, and after a minute I went to my own room. The last I saw of Count Dracula was a red light of triumph in his eyes and a diabolical smile.

As I was about to lie down in bed, I thought I heard a whispering outside my door. And then the voice of the Count.

"Back! Back to your own place! Your time is not yet come! Wait. Have patience. Tomorrow night, the night is yours."

There was a low, sweet ripple of laughter. In a rage, I flung back the door and saw the three terrible women licking their lips. As they saw me, they all joined in a horrible laugh, and ran away.

I fell on my knees and prayed: "Lord, help me, and those who love me!"

Tomorrow! Is that to be the end?

June 30

These may be the last words I ever write in my diary. I woke before dawn, when it was still dark. Again I sank to my knees and prayed, for I thought, if Death comes, I shall be found ready.

Then I felt a subtle change in the air, and knew that morning had broken. I heard the welcome sound of the rooster crowing, and I knew I was safe. With a feeling of gladness, I opened my door and ran down to the hall. Escape was before me. My hands trembling with eagerness, I unhooked the chains and drew back the massive bolts.

But the door would not move. Despair seized me. I pulled at the door, till, massive as it was, it rattled, and then I could see… it was locked. The Count must have locked it after I left him last night.

Then a wild feeling shot through me. I had to get that key, whatever the risk. I decided to climb down the wall and enter the Count's room. He might kill me, but death seemed the happier choice of evils. Without a pause, I rushed back to my room, then opening the window, scrambled down the wall, as before.

The Count's room was empty, as I expected. I could not see the key anywhere, but the heap of gold was still there. I went through the door in the corner and down the winding stair and along the dark passage to the old chapel.

I knew where the monster would be.

The box was in the same place, with the lid on it, and nails were ready in their places to be hammered down. I raised the lid, and there was the Count.

His appearance filled me with horror. He looked as if half his youth had been renewed. His white hair had become darker, now more iron than silver. His cheeks were fuller, the skin on his face seemed pinker, and his mouth was redder than ever, for on the lips were blobs of fresh blood, which trickled from the corners of his mouth and ran over his chin and neck. Even his eyelids and the pouches under his eyes were bloated. It looked as if he was gorged with blood.

He lay like a filthy leech, exhausted by his feeding. I shuddered as I bent over to touch him. I was revolted, but I had to search, or I was doomed.

I felt all over the body, but no sign could I find of the key. When I looked at his face, there was a mocking smile on it, which drove me mad. This was the creature I had agreed to help buy a house just outside London, a city of teeming millions, where he would come, perhaps for hundreds of years, to suck blood from the helpless, and create ever-widening circles of demons. I wanted, more than anything else in the world, to kill him. To rid the world of such a monster. But no lethal weapon was at hand. I seized a shovel, which was all I could find, and struck it at the hateful face.

As I did so, the face turned and the eyes fell full on me with all their blaze of stony horror. I had gashed him on the forehead; that was all. As the shovel slipped from my grasp, it hit the lid of the box, which closed upon the Count. The last glimpse I had of him was his bloated face, bloodstained, fixed with a grin of pure malice.

I thought and thought about my next move. Despair swept over me. With a last look at the box containing that vile body, I ran from the chapel, back to the Count's room.

…I heard somewhere in the castle a gypsy song, sung by merry voices. The gypsies had come back then. Evidently, they were working for the Count, for now I heard their tramping feet, the clanking of heavy weights, the grinding of the key in the lock, the drawing back of chains and bolts. I strained my ears, listening and waiting for the moment I could escape.

In the courtyard, I heard the crack of whips and the roll of heavy wheels. They were leaving… gone, passing into the distance.

I tried the Count's door. Locked. I turned to run

back to the vault – there might, I reasoned, be another door down there that led outside. But at that moment, there was a violent gust of wind, and the door that led to the winding stair blew shut. When I tried to push it open, it stuck, hopelessly shut fast.

I am again a prisoner. The net of doom is closing around me more closely. I am alone in the castle with those awful women. Oh! Mina is a woman, but has nothing in common with those demons.

I shall not stay here. I shall try to climb the castle wall further than I have yet done. I shall take some of the gold with me. I may need it, if I find a way from this dreadful place.

And then away for home! Away to the quickest and nearest train! Away from this cursed spot where the devil walks the land.

If I fall to my death, then sleep is mine as a man, not as the Count's victim.

Goodbye all! Mina!

CHAPTER 4
LOVELY LUCY

MINA'S JOURNAL

MAY 9

My friend Lucy and I are having a holiday by the
sea at Whitby. Lucy has just become engaged to
Arthur. What a girl she is! She charms everyone, and she
is so pretty. Arthur's friend, that clever man, Dr. Seward,
I think was a little in love with her too, but Lucy's heart
belongs to Arthur. If only Jonathan were here, I would
feel perfectly happy. I have not heard from him, which
worries me. He is usually so good at writing to me. He is
a perfect fiancé, and will be the best of husbands.

July 26

Still no news of Jonathan.

I wrote to Mr. Hawkins, to see if he had heard anything, and he forwarded me a letter he'd received from Jonathan from Castle Dracula, saying he was just starting for home. It did not sound like Jonathan, and I am uneasy.

Lucy has begun to walk in her sleep. I do not like this either.

August 3

Still no news of Jonathan. I hope he isn't ill. Surely he would have told me.

August 6

Still no news. There has been a terrible storm, the wind roaring like thunder, the waves mountain high, and the horizon disappearing in mist. In the sea fog, sadly, a tragic shipwreck emerged, swept onto the shore. Every man aboard had been washed away, drowned, save for the captain. He was a corpse with a drooping head, lashed to the ship's wheel. The ship's cargo was brought ashore. It was a strange cargo. Everyone was talking about it – even the local papers. It contained fifty boxes of soil.

I was glad Jonathan was not at sea last night. But where is he? If only I knew.

AUGUST 8

We have had such an agonizing experience. I woke suddenly last night, in a state of unexplained fear. I looked at Lucy in her bed, but she was not there. Her dressing gown was hanging on the back of the door, and the front door was open. There was only one explanation: she had to be sleepwalking – outside, in her white nightdress. I grabbed a shawl and ran to find her.

At last in the churchyard on the cliff top, in the silvery light of the moon, I saw a snowy-white figure. Lucy! It seemed to me that something dark was bent over her. As I hurried nearer, I saw this thing had a face with red gleaming eyes, but when I got to her she was alone. She was still asleep. She was breathing in gasps, as if trying to fill her lungs. I woke her gently, putting the shawl around her, but she put her hands to her throat with a moan. She came back with me obediently. She seemed not at all surprised to see me.

I have decided to lock the door of our bedroom at night.

Lucy is to marry Arthur in the autumn. She is already making great plans. Arthur is coming to Whitby soon (his father is not well – he will come as soon as he can leave him) and Lucy is counting the minutes till he arrives. She wants to take him up to the seat on the churchyard cliff. I expect it is all this waiting that disturbs her.

SAME DAY. NOON.

Lucy slept all morning, and seems better. I saw she had two little red marks on her throat and on the band of her nightdress is a drop of blood. I must have caught her with an unseen pin when I wrapped her in the shawl.

AUGUST 13

Another quiet day. We went for a walk, and Lucy made a strange remark. We were looking at the view over the cliff from our seat in the churchyard, when she said, "His red eyes again!" She seemed to be in a half-dreamy state with an odd look on her face. I said nothing, but followed her eyes and saw, for an instant, a dark figure on the seat with great eyes like burning flames. The sun was setting, reflecting in the bright stained-glass panes of the church windows, so perhaps it was all an illusion. And perhaps Lucy was thinking of that terrible night of sleepwalking. She had a headache and went early to bed.

I went for a walk. Coming back, I saw Lucy leaning out of the bedroom window. I thought she was looking at me, and waved, but she took no notice. As I got closer, I saw distinctly in the moonlight that she was lying with her eyes shut against the side of the windowsill. By her, seated on the windowsill, was a large bird. I was afraid she'd catch a chill, so I ran upstairs, but as I came into the room, she was moving back to bed, breathing heavily, holding her hand to her throat.

She looked paler than usual and there is an exhausted, worn-down look under her eyes. She must be fretting about something.

AUGUST 15

Lucy is not well. She is pale and weak… she grows weaker every day. At night I hear her gasping for air. The tiny wounds on her throat are still open, and, if anything, larger than before.

I do not understand why she is fading away.

Still nothing from Jonathan.

AUGUST 19

Joy! Though not all joy. At last, news of Jonathan. He has been ill. Mr. Hawkins wrote to tell me he is in a hospital in Buda-Pesth. I am going out there straight away to help nurse him back to health. Perhaps we may even be married out there. Lucy is a little better, and her mother is coming to Whitby to look after her.

AUGUST 24

My poor Jonathan! I have arrived in Buda-Pesth after a long journey, which I hardly remember, my mind being full of Jonathan. I went by train from Whitby to Hull, caught the boat to Hamburg, and then found a train to take me on to here.

Jonathan has been very ill, with brain fever. I found my dear one, oh, so thin and weak and pale-looking. Sister Agatha, a sweet, good woman and a born nurse, who has been looking after him, told me he has been raving about dreadful things, but refuses to tell me what, saying the ravings of the sick are the secrets of God. He does not remember anything that has happened to him for a long time past. At least, this is what he wants me to believe, and I shall never ask. All Sister Agatha would say was: "You, as his wife-to-be, have no need to worry. He has never forgotten you. His fear was of great and terrible things which no mortal can understand."

We are to be married very soon. He says that the thought of our wedding makes him recover faster than anything. He gave me a notebook. In it, he said, he had written down the terrible events that brought on his fever. He did not want to remember them. He did not even know if they were true or dreams. He wanted our marriage to be as if life were beginning afresh.

"Never tell me if you read it," he said, "unless, out of duty, I am forced to go back to those bitter hours."

I took the book, tied it up with ribbon and sealed the knot with sealing wax. I told him I would keep it as a sign that we trusted each other, and would never open it unless I had to, for the sake of duty.

LUCY'S DIARY

AUGUST 24

I am back at home, with my mother. I must be like Mina, and write everything down, so we can have long talks when we meet. I wish she were with me, for I feel so unhappy. I've been dreaming again, as I did at Whitby. Every night, I hear a sort of scratching or flapping at my window, and then I have more bad dreams. I feel horribly weak, and my throat hurts. I don't ever seem to get enough air. I shall have to cheer up when Arthur comes, or he will be miserable to see me so.

LETTER FROM ARTHUR TO DR. SEWARD
AUGUST 31

Dear Jack,

Please help me out. I have been staying with Lucy and her mother, but now I have to visit my father, who is ill. I am anxious about Lucy. She has no particular disease, but she looks awful and is getting worse every day. Please come and see her, and tell me what you think.

LETTER FROM DR. SEWARD TO ARTHUR
SEPTEMBER 3

Dear Arthur,

I am puzzled. Lucy is somewhat bloodless, perhaps low in iron, and complains of bad dreams. I have asked my old friend, Professor Van Helsing from Amsterdam, to see her. He is one of the cleverest scientists, and a wise and good man.

DR. SEWARD'S DIARY

SEPTEMBER 7

Arthur has returned from his father's bedside, and we are both very concerned about Lucy. Van Helsing is equally puzzled. Today, her deterioration has been rapid. She is ghostly pale, almost unconscious, and her breathing is painful.

"There is no time to be lost," said Van Helsing. "She will die from sheer want of blood to keep the heart going. She must have a blood transfusion."

"Let me give mine," exclaimed Arthur. "I would gladly give my last drop for her!"

Van Helsing gave Lucy a narcotic, and swiftly, but with absolute method, performed the operation. The loss of blood weakened Arthur slightly, but he is a strong young man, and will recover fast. Soon Lucy's cheeks returned to a healthier shade of pink, and her breathing was easier. As I watched her, I saw that the velvet band she wore around her throat had dragged up, revealing a red mark.

"What do you make of that?" I asked.

There were two punctures, not large, but not good, either.

The Professor stood up.

"I must go to Amsterdam at once," he said. "There are books there that I must consult. You must watch over Lucy all night. Do not sleep. Arthur is too weak to take his post. I shall be back as soon as I can, and then we may begin."

"Begin what?" I asked.

"We shall see," he answered, hurrying out.

I sat up with Lucy all night. She did not want to sleep. She said she was afraid, but when I promised her I would be there, she dropped off, saying with a deep sigh of relief, "No more bad dreams then."

SEPTEMBER 10

Lucy seemed so much better that I saw no need to sit with her again. I fell asleep myself in the day, as I was so tired. I was eventually woken by the Professor, back from Amsterdam. Together we visited our patient.

55

"Good heavens!" hissed the Professor, pointing to the bed.

There lay poor Lucy, more horribly white than ever. Even her lips were white, the gums shrunken back from the teeth, like a corpse. All our work had been undone.

I was already rolling up my sleeve, ready to give my blood, while Van Helsing took the instruments for the operation out of his bag. He acted swiftly, and I saw her cheeks become pink again.

"Is that all?" I asked. "You took more blood from Arthur."

"He is her fiancé, that is why. That will suffice, for the moment, for you have much, much work to do…"

My thoughts came back to the two little punctures in her throat, and the ragged appearance of their edges.

Van Helsing went out for a walk, and came back with a great armful of garlic flowers. Some of these he kept aside. He fastened the windows in Lucy's room, rubbing the flowers all over the panes and the window frames, and all over the door – as though to ensure that every whiff of air that came in would be saturated with the smell. The rest of the flowers he wove into a wreath and hung them around Lucy's neck.

"Do not take it off," he told her. "And do not open the window tonight, or the door."

"I promise," said Lucy. "I never liked garlic before, but it feels peaceful. I feel a sense of comfort. I shall sleep well tonight."

SEPTEMBER 13

For the first time, I saw Van Helsing in despair.

As we were about to climb the stairs to check on Lucy, her mother came out of the sitting room with a look of delight on her face.

"Lucy is so much better – because of me!" she said. "Her room was so stuffy, I opened her windows, and all those horrible, strong-smelling flowers around her neck were so oppressive I took them away. I am sure you will be pleased."

When she'd left us, Van Helsing raised his arms as though appealing to the whole universe.

"What have we done? How are all the powers of the devils against us? This poor mother acts for the best, all unknowing… we must fight on."

Together we went up to Lucy's room. Her waxen face lay unconscious. This time, Van Helsing gave his blood, and after an hour, Lucy awoke, seemingly fresh and bright.

What does it all mean?

SEPTEMBER 18

I have read a strange story in the newspaper, about a wolf that escaped from London Zoo, terrorizing the inhabitants of London, and then returning to the zoo that night, with his head cut and full of broken glass.

LUCY'S DIARY

UNDATED

I feel I am dying of weakness. But I must record what happened tonight.

I went to bed as usual and fell asleep quickly, but was wakened by a flapping at the window – something I've heard often since sleepwalking at Whitby. I tried to go back to sleep, but could not. Then, outside I heard a sort of howl, like a dog, but more fierce. I went to the window and looked out, but I could see nothing except a big bat which must have been hitting its wings against the window. The door opened, and Mother came in, saying, "I heard you moving about. Are you all right?"

Dear mother! We hugged, and then the flapping at the window came again. Then there was a crash, and a lot of broken glass was hurled at the floor. The wind rushed in and between the broken panes was the great, gaunt head of a wolf. Mother sat up and pointed, crying out in fright. There was a strange and horrible gurgling in her throat, and then she fell over as if struck by lightning. The wolf drew his head back, and a whole myriad of little speckles seemed to come blowing through the broken window, wheeling like dust.

I tried to move, but it was as if a spell had been cast upon me. I could not move. My poor mother's body grew cold. Her heart had stopped.

What am I to do? God shield me from harm. Goodbye, dear Arthur, if I do not survive this night. God keep you, and God help me.

Dr. Seward's Diary
September 19

A terrible time. The Professor, Arthur and I came back to the house. A scene of horror awaited us. Glass on the floor. Lucy's mother: dead. Shock, I think. Lucy lay on her bed, her face as white as her pillow. She was breathing loudly, her face at its worst, for the open mouth showed pale gums. Her teeth seemed longer and sharper. In particular, by some trick of the light, her canine teeth looked longer and sharper than the rest.

Van Helsing looked at her throat. "The wounds have disappeared," he said, in a voice of calm yet despair. "She is dying. It will not be long now."

Arthur covered his face with his hands and slid to his knees, praying, while his shoulders shook with grief. Then he came to her bedside. She opened her eyes, and seeing him, whispered softly, "Arthur! Oh my love!"

He was stooping to kiss her when Van Helsing held him back. "No!" he whispered. "Hold her hand."

Lucy sank into sleep. She looked her best, the soft lines of her face falling into angelic beauty. And then a change crept over her. The mouth opened, the lips dropped back, showing her sharp teeth. In a sort of sleep-waking way, she opened her eyes, which were now hard, and in a soft urging voice, utterly unlike her own, murmured, "Arthur! Kiss me!"

Arthur stooped again, but Van Helsing dragged him away, crying, "No! Not for your living soul and hers!"

A spasm of rage flitted over her face. Then we heard her real voice, as she said with pathos,

"Guard him, my friends, and give him peace." Her breathing grew harsh, and then ceased altogether.

Arthur broke down, sobbing pitifully.

"Ah, poor girl, there is peace for her now," I said.

"Not so," replied Van Helsing. "It is only the beginning."

When I asked him what he meant, he shook his head. "We can do nothing yet. Wait and see."

We have arranged for her to be buried tomorrow, with her mother.

We tried to make the sad proceedings as beautiful as possible, strewing Lucy's body with flowers. With every moment that passed, her loveliness increased, so that Arthur echoed my own thoughts when he said:

"Is she really dead?"

It was hard to believe that a corpse lay there. The Professor looked sternly grave as he laid upon her a handful of wild garlic and a crucifix.

CHAPTER 5
THE UNDEAD

MINA'S DIARY
SEPTEMBER 22

I have my husband back. Recovered, but still weak. He still has nightmares, and he fears that this is a sign of madness. Poor Jonathan. We are back in England. We had to come quickly. We had a telegram saying Mr. Hawkins, his senior partner, is dead. Jonathan is now head of the law firm. We are in London to arrange Mr. Hawkins's funeral.

As we walked down Piccadilly earlier today, Jonathan suddenly gripped my arm tightly. I am always anxious about him, but when I looked at him, his eyes were bulging in terror and amazement. He was gazing at a tall man with black hair, who was observing a pretty girl. I had a good look at the man. His face was hard and cruel. His big white teeth looked all the whiter because his lips were so red.

"Am I mad? I believe that is the Count, but he has grown young," said Jonathan.

As we watched, the man followed the girl, and both disappeared from sight.

LATER

This is a sad homecoming. We have received a telegram telling us of the deaths of Lucy and her mother. Poor Arthur, to have lost the sweetness of his life. Lucy is buried in Hampstead Hill, where the air blows fresh and the wild flowers grow.

Jonathan had a bad night, but is better today, back at work. I have read of such strange events in this morning's newspaper. Several children around Hampstead have been missing at night. They are found in the morning, weak and emaciated, all with small wounds in their throats, such as might have been made by a rat or a dog.

I have had a letter from Professor Van Helsing, who was with Lucy at her death. He wants to see me urgently, and I sent a telegram to arrange his visit later today.

SEPTEMBER 23

The Professor has come and gone. My thoughts are in a whirl. I showed him Jonathan's diary that I had sealed up. I read it too, with ever-increasing shock. How Jonathan must have suffered. The Professor was profoundly grateful to be shown it, saying that all the facts that he had surmised were now proved without doubt.

I am relieved. The notebook proves that Jonathan was never mad. His ravings were based on things that actually happened. Terrible, nightmarish, fearful events. Jonathan will be relieved too. The fear that he was mad has been haunting him.

But the Professor wants even more certain proof. He read the article in my newspaper, about the children in Hampstead with small puncture wounds in their throats. He says this needs investigation, and that it is to do with Lucy. He wants Jonathan and Arthur to join him and go to Lucy's grave.

DR. SEWARD'S DIARY
SEPTEMBER 24

Van Helsing told me that the holes in the throats of these young children were made by Lucy.

I was very angry. I hit the table, exclaiming, "Are you mad?" I did not believe him.

We met again that night, in the churchyard, the four of us, Mina, Jonathan, Van Helsing and me. No one else was about. Arthur looked grim. I was sceptical, but Jonathan appeared full of relief, and Mina's face was set with courage. Van Helsing lit a candle, and in its meagre light we went down into the vault.

When we were last there, to bury Lucy and her mother, it was daytime. The vault had looked desolate, even though the flowers on Lucy's tomb were fresh, but now, at night, some days later, the blossoms hung lank and dead. Spiders and beetles had made their home amongst the dusty mortar and rusted iron.

Van Helsing unscrewed the coffin lid, and lifted it up. The coffin was empty.

"That proves nothing," I said. "Maybe a body-snatcher has removed the body."

"Then we will have more proof. Come," said the Professor. We followed him into the churchyard, where, lying on the grass was a tiny sleeping child.

"Are you satisfied now?" he asked.

"No," I said aggressively.

He examined the child's throat. It was unmarked.

"Thank God we are just in time," said the Professor. "We will take this child now to Hampstead Heath, and leave it where it will be found by a policeman. If we take it directly to the police, we will have to make some sort of statement as to how and where we found it, and we do not want that."

We went to the Heath, and at its edge, we heard the heavy tread of a policeman. We laid the child on the path, waiting until he saw it as he swung his lantern to and fro. We heard his exclamation of astonishment, as he carried it safely away.

We returned to the vault. Once again, Van Helsing forced back the coffin lid.

There lay Lucy, if possible even more radiantly beautiful. I could not believe she was dead. The lips were redder than before, and on the cheeks was a delicate bloom.

"Are you convinced now?" asked the Professor. As he spoke, he pulled back the lips and showed the teeth.

"See," he said. "They are sharper than before. With this…" he touched one of the canines, "little children can be bitten. Most people would not look as she does after death. She is one of the Undead."

"Undead? What do you mean?" cried Arthur. "Has she been buried alive?"

"No. She is in the trance of the Undead. She craves blood. That was why I would not let Arthur kiss her. She would have bitten him. The only way to release her from her trance is to kill her."

"No! You can't! To desecrate her who I loved…" Arthur's voice choked with grief and horror.

"I assure you, it is the only way," said the Professor, with a pitying look. "Tomorrow night, we will meet again, here."

"I cannot let you," repeated Arthur. "I do not understand, but I must come with you tomorrow."

The following night, at midnight, we went to the churchyard. Occasional gleams of moonlight lit the dark sky. The air was sweet and fresh, compared to the terror that awaited us in the vault.

Van Helsing led the way with a lantern, and again opened the coffin. Again, it was empty. He closed the lid, and waited.

Around us, the other tombs looked ghostly white. Never did the sounds of the night seem more ominous… the rustling of trees… the far-off howling of dogs.

"See…" said the Professor, pointing.

We saw a dim white figure advance in the moonlight, dressed in the clothes of the grave. It was holding a fair-haired child, a little boy. Arthur gave a gasp of horror, and I felt my own heart grow chill. It was Lucy.

Van Helsing held up his lantern as she drew closer. We could see her sweet features had turned to cruelty, her purity to graspingness, her soft eyes harden. Worse still, her lips were crimson with blood, which trickled down her chin and stained her clothes.

When she saw Arthur, she flung the child down, and stretched out her arms.

"Come to me."

Never had her voice sounded more alluring.

Van Helsing held up his crucifix, and the figure

recoiled in rage. The lovely, blood-stained mouth became a square of passion. If ever a face meant death, we saw it in that moment, as she dashed past to re-enter the tomb.

"Is it a demon in her shape?" asked Arthur? "Or is it really Lucy?"

"Let me explain more. The Undead are cursed with immortality. They must go on, sucking blood, creating more victims, who then crave blood themselves, and so the circle becomes ever wider. This poor lady is a young Undead. She does not suck much blood, but as time goes on, she will take more and more. But if she is sent to her rest, as truly dead, her soul will be free. It will be a blessed relief for her. I am prepared to do this deed, but the one who loved her has a better right."

Arthur's hand trembled, but he stepped forward bravely. "Tell me what I must do, and I shall do it, to restore Lucy to holiness."

We looked at the tomb. Lucy had returned to it, lying there in all her beauty. Van Helsing handed

Arthur a stake and a hammer, and began to read a prayer for the dead from the Prayer Book.

Arthur's courage never faltered. He struck. The Thing in the coffin writhed and shook in wild contortions, and a hideous, blood-curdling screech came from the mouth.

Finally the body lay still, no longer the foul being, but Lucy again, dead, yes, but pure and sweet. God's true dead, whose soul was with Him.

Van Helsing picked up the child who lay asleep on the grass.

"No harm has come to this little one. We will leave him where he will be found, safe and well. We have done the first step of our work, but there remains a greater task.

CHAPTER 6

BLOOD LUST IN LONDON

MINA'S DIARY

OCTOBER 1

I have told the Professor everything I remember: Lucy's bad dreams, and the shipwreck that came ashore with fifty boxes of soil. He said Dracula was evidently on that ship, taking the shape of a bat to attack Lucy. He said, too, that I have helped him in his research into vampires.

Jonathan has managed to trace some of those boxes. Dracula had arranged for them to be delivered to Carfax. Not all of the fifty are there.

We must find them all and destroy them, the Professor says. We do this by sprinkling them with holy water.

I understand everything now. The Professor has explained. We must be serious, yet business-like. We have a job to do. It felt as if we had formed ourselves into some sort of committee.

This is what the Professor said:

"Dracula is a vampire. The history of vampires is the stuff of superstition and tradition. They are known everywhere, in ancient Greece and Rome, Germany, France, China… they live amongst the Slav, the Saxon, the Magyar. We know they never die. When they kill, they get stronger. They fatten on the blood of the living. This one, Dracula, is more cunning than mortals. He has power over the dead. He can appear at will in any form he chooses – as a bat, a fox, a wolf. He can direct the elements: the storm, thunder, fog. He comes on moonlight rays as elemental dust. He can become small, as Lucy did when she slipped back into her tomb.

"He is not entirely free. His power ceases in the day. He can only change himself at noon, or sunrise and sunset. He rests in his daylight hours of inactivity in his earth boxes… his lair. Then there are things that he cannot stand. Garlic, a crucifix, a bullet fired into his coffin, or a stake driven into his heart. If we can find him there, we must destroy him. If we fail in our fight, he will surely win. Then we will become like him, a blot on the face of God's sunshine, without heart or conscience. What do you say?"

We all agreed to do all we could to rid the world of Dracula. Solemnly, we shook hands on our pact.

The others are going to Carfax. Tonight.

JONATHAN HARKER'S JOURNAL
OCTOBER 2
It is such a dread to me that Mina is mixed up in this business. The Professor wanted her to stay behind while the rest of us went to Carfax, and she consented, with reluctance.

We made our way there by moonlight. We took care to hide in the shadows of the trees in the garden. When we got to the porch, the Professor opened his bag, and took out a little silver crucifix, a wreath of garlic, a revolver and a knife. These he divided up amongst us. He also produced a random collection of keys, all of which he tried in the lock, so that we need not break into the house.

At last he found one to suit. The Professor was the first to step forward, crossing himself as he passed over the threshold, with the words *In manus tuas, Domine*. 'In your hands, Lord'. Then we all lit our lanterns, and began our search.

The light from these lamps fell in odd forms as the rays crossed each other, and our bodies threw shadows. I kept feeling someone else was there. The others must have thought so too, for I noticed they kept looking over their shoulders with every new shadow, as I did.

The whole place was thick with dust. The floor was inches deep in it, except in some places where

I could see recent footsteps. The walls, too, were thick and fluffy with it, and in the corners were masses of spiders' webs, on which the dust had gathered till they looked like bunches of rags. On a table in the hall was a great bunch of keys.

The Professor turned to me.

"You know this place, Jonathan. You have copied maps of it. Which is the way to the chapel?"

I led them till we reached a low, arched door, ribbed with iron bands. We found the right key, and opened the door, locking it behind us.

A terrible smell hit our nostrils. How can I describe it? The chapel was small and close, and long disuse had made the air stagnant and foul. But this smell was far more horrible than that. It had the pungent smell of blood, as well as an earthy smell, as of some dry miasma… it seemed to be made of all the ills of humanity, as if corruption had fed upon itself.

In ordinary circumstances, such a stench would have brought about our hasty exit, but our purpose gave us added strength. We set about our work as though that loathsome place were a garden of roses.

We examined every nook and cranny. There were the boxes of soil. We counted… twenty-nine. Twenty-one were missing.

Arthur said suddenly, "I thought I saw a face."

We all looked, and in the shadows I seemed to glimpse the Count's face, his red eyes, his red lips, his awful paleness. I turned my lamp in that direction, but saw no one. As there were no windows, no door except the one we had entered by, which was now locked, there could be no hiding place, even for him. Dr. Seward stepped back. We were all nervous now.

Then, before our eyes was a whole mass of phosphorescence, twinkling like stars, and suddenly the place was overrun with rats. Every minute, their numbers increased, swarming everywhere at once, till the lamplight, shining on their glittering eyes, made the place look like a nest of fireflies.

Arthur was prepared for such an emergency. He unlocked the door, and, taking a whistle from his pocket, blew it shrilly and loudly. Three stray dogs dashed in, yelping at the rats, tossing them in the air with vicious shakes, chasing them. In a trice, the whole plague vanished.

Our spirits lifted, as though some evil presence had departed. The dogs frisked about, just as if they had been doing nothing more disturbing than rabbit-hunting in a summer wood.

By this time, the dawn was breaking in the east. It was time to leave Carfax, locking all the doors behind us. The Professor was pleased with our night's expedition.

"We have seen," he said, "that though the rats came at the Count's call, they fled from the dogs. He was not here tonight. It is like a game of chess, which we play for the sake of human souls. We have cried 'check' in some way tonight."

…I returned home to find Mina asleep in bed. I was so exhausted I slept till noon, and she must have been tired too, for I had to wake her. She was so sound asleep that at first she did not seem to recognize me, but looked around with a blank terror, as if waking from a bad dream.

MINA'S DIARY

OCTOBER 2

I feel strangely sad today.

Jonathan did not tell me a word of what went on at Carfax last night, though he spoke to me so sweetly and tenderly. I know he does not want to worry me, but it still saddens me that he does not take me into his confidence as he always has.

I've been thinking over everything that has happened. I am always anxious. Oh, why did I ever go to Whitby? If I hadn't, perhaps Lucy would be with us now. She might not have started walking in her sleep, and if she hadn't gone to the churchyard, the monster might not have found her. There now, crying again! I keep crying. I wonder what has come over me.

Last night, before I fell asleep, I heard the sound of dogs barking, and then a silence so profound that I got up and looked out of the window. All the dark shadows thrown by the moonlight seemed full of mystery, fixed grim as death. As I stared, I saw a thin streak – a white mist creeping slowly towards the house. It spread, up to my window, which I shut. I went back to bed, frightened, pulling the covers over my ears.

I must have fallen asleep and, I suppose, dreamt that I thought I was asleep and waiting for Jonathan to come back. I was very worried about him. Then it began to dawn on me that the air was dank and cold. The fog had somehow got in through the window which I was sure I'd shut. I wanted to check, but I was overcome by such overpowering leaden lethargy that I couldn't move. The mist was like smoke. I could see it now coming through the joinings of the door. It whirled, growing thicker and thicker till it was like a column, and then it divided, and I seemed to see in it two red eyes, just as Lucy described in her wanderings on the cliff. Then I remembered that it was thus that Jonathan had seen those awful women becoming more and more real through the whirling mist in the moonlight. The last thing I remember before sleep overcame me was a white face bending over me.

JONATHAN HARKER'S JOURNAL

OCTOBER 3

I have been busy doing research all over London, asking all the cab drivers if they have carried any heavy boxes full of soil. At last – success! I found a cab driver, a Mr. Smollet, a very decent, intelligent workman, who gave me the information I sought. He remembered all about the boxes. He had been hired to take six to 127, Chicksand Street, near Mile End Road, and another six to Jamaica Lane, Bermondsey. That was to the east and the south. Bearing Carfax in mind, I worked out that the Count could not really have wanted to confine himself to three sides of London, east, south and north. His diabolical scheme must also have included the west. I gave Mr. Smollet a generous tip, to see if he could give me any more information.

He racked his brains, and remembered a friend of his who had taken nine boxes from Carfax to a house in Piccadilly. I went to see this friend who told me an old man with white hair was waiting for him at Carfax. The man was so strong that he tossed the heavy boxes into the cart as if they weighed no more than feathers. When the cart-driver got to Piccadilly, the old man, strangely, was already there. My new friend couldn't remember the number of the house, but said it was a dusty old place, with steep steps leading up to its door.

That was enough for me. I researched estate agents and found that 347 Piccadilly had been bought by a foreign nobleman, Count de Ville, who had paid for his purchase in cash. I then went to tell Van Helsing and Arthur all I had learned.

"Well done," said the Professor. "If we find all those missing boxes, our work will be drawing to an end. But then we must hunt the wretch until his death."

"How are we to get into the house in Piccadilly?" I wondered.

"We break in, as we did at Carfax," said Arthur.

"But this is different, Arthur," I said. "At Carfax we had the night and large empty grounds to protect us. It will be a mighty different thing to commit a burglary in the middle of Piccadilly."

I went back home. Mina was asleep; her forehead was puckered up into little wrinkles, as if she were thinking even in her dreams. She looks pale, even a little haggard. Tomorrow, I hope, will mend all this.

Dr. Seward's Diary
October 4

Terrible, terrible. I went to have tea with Mina. Mina was not herself. She was like tea, weak, after the tea had been watered. She spoke of a mist that had appeared in her bedroom the previous evening.

I could not rest for worry. I could not sleep, though the hour was late. I went around to Van Helsing and Arthur, and urged them to accompany me to the Harkers. Naturally, they were eager to help. We took with us the same items we had when we entered Carfax.

"Alas! Alas that Mina should suffer!" said the Professor. "We must enter their bedroom, even if the door is locked. If the door does not open, we must press our shoulders against it and shove."

"Won't it frighten her, if we burst in?" asked Arthur.

"This is life and death."

We almost fell headlong into the room, as the door opened with a crash under our pressure – and met an appalling sight.

Bright moonlight lit the scene. On the bed lay Jonathan, breathing heavily, as though in a stupor. Kneeling by the bed was the white-clad figure of his wife. By her side was a tall, thin man, dressed in black. With his left hand, he gripped Mina's hands; his right hand had grabbed the back of her neck, forcing it against his chest. Her nightgown was smeared with blood, and more blood trickled down his chest.

Yes, it was the Count. He looked at us with his fiendish red eyes, flaming with passion, his mouth snarling, showing his white sharp teeth.

He threw his victim back on the bed and sprang at us. The Professor instantly held up his crucifix – Arthur and I held up ours too – and the Count cowered back. The moonlight suddenly faded, and we saw nothing but a faint streak of mist, which shrank out of the door.

Mina let out a scream so wild, so ear-piercing, so despairing, that it will ring in my ears until my dying day. Her face was ghastly pale, accentuated by the blood on her lips, cheeks and chin; her eyes mad with terror. Then she covered her face with her hands and moaned. She tried hard to recover herself, turning to her husband with her arms stretched out as though to hug him. Then she stopped herself, shuddering.

Jonathan woke up from his stupor, exclaiming, "What is this! What has happened? Mina, what does all that blood mean?" He began to pull on his clothes, crying, "Oh, do something to save her! Guard her while I look for him!"

She seized him, pleading, "No, do not leave me. I have suffered enough tonight, God knows, without dread of his harming you too." She clung to him fiercely, staining his nightrobe with blood.

The Professor held out his crucifix.

"My dear, you are safe enough tonight, and while this is close, no foul thing can harm you."

But Mina had seen the red marks on Jonathan's nightrobe, and drew back, sobbing.

"I am unclean! I must touch him no more! I am now his worst enemy!"

"Nonsense, Mina. Never speak like that," said Jonathan, folding her into his arms, his mouth set as steel. With studied calmness, he asked, as her sobs grew less, "What happened?"

"I went to sleep," she said bravely, making an effort to speak, "but my sleep was disturbed by dreams of vampires and endless horrors."

Jonathan groaned, and she turned to him, saying, "Do not fret, dearest. You must be strong and brave and help me. Well, I woke, feeling the same vague fear that I'd felt before, while the room filled with white mist. You were asleep by my side, sleeping so soundly that I could not wake you. That terrified me. Then I saw beside the bed – as if he had stepped out of the mist – a tall, thin man in black. I knew who he was, from the descriptions of him, and the red eyes were those I had seemed to see in sunset on the windows of the church at Whitby. I would have screamed, but he said in a hissing whisper:

"Silence! If you make a sound, I shall dash his brains out as you watch." With a mocking smile, he bared my throat saying, "First, a little refreshment to reward my journey. This is not the first time, or the second, that your veins have quenched my thirst." I was bewildered, but powerless to stop him. I suppose this is part of the curse that happens when he touches a victim. And then, oh, pity me! He put his foul lips on my throat."

Jonathan groaned again, as if he were the one injured. She stroked him, trying to comfort him, and went on:

"I felt my strength fading away. I don't know how long it lasted, but it seemed a long time. Then he said, "So! I know you would like to pit your brains against mine. You want to help these men hunt me. Me! I who have fought against those like them for hundreds of years before they were born… who have commanded nations – and won. You, the best-beloved of one of them, are now my flesh and blood, and shall later on be my helper. Now, you shall come whenever I call. When my brain says, "Come!" you will cross land and sea to do my bidding. And to make that happen – ah! This!"

"With that, he pulled open his shirt, and with his long, sharp nails, opened a vein in his chest. When the blood began to spurt out, he pressed my mouth to the wound so hard that I must either drink or suffocate. What have I done? Why has this happened to me? I have tried all my life to be good, and now…"

She wiped her lips as though attempting to cleanse them from pollution. Her husband stood by her, his face pale, his hair whitening with shock. The sun was rising, morning light spread its kindly beams, but it lit no more miserable house than this in all its great round of daily course.

Chapter 7
Mark Of Evil

Jonathan Harker's Journal

October 5

I shall go mad if I do not write my diary. Poor Mina. She is so brave. She said last night that we must keep trusting in God, who will help us in the end. Then she told us, tears running down her cheeks, that she had made up her mind.

"To what?" asked Van Helsing, very gently, for I think we all had an idea what she meant.

Her answer was simple.

"If I find in myself any symptom – like Lucy

suffered – that will harm those I love, I shall die."

"You would not kill yourself?" he asked.

"I would, if there were no one who could help me… who could save me…"

Van Helsing sat beside her and took her hand. "You must not die. Don't you see, your death would make you one of the Undead, as Dracula is. No, you must live! You must struggle and strive for life, even if death seems preferable. You must not die, nor think of death, while this great evil is upon us."

Mina shook and shivered. We could do nothing but silently support her, till she grew more calm, and gave her word.

"I promise that I shall try to live, if God will let me, and trust that this horror will pass."

As usual Van Helsing was thinking ahead and making plans.

"It is a good thing that we did nothing with the earth-boxes when we went to Carfax. If we had, Dracula would have guessed our purpose, and would have removed the others. He does not know

92

our intentions, nor does he realize we have power to sterilize his lairs. When we go to the house in Piccadilly, we will have tracked the last of the boxes. Today, then, is ours, and in it rests our hope. Until sunset tonight, Dracula is mortal. He cannot melt into thin air nor reappear in mist. We have the whole day to hunt for the earth-boxes. It is likely that the keys for the houses in Bermondsey and Mile End are in the Piccadilly house. It is so central that he can come and go without anyone noticing him. We will go there now, sterilize all the earth-boxes, and then find the Count."

"Quick! Let's go now," I cried. "We're wasting time. Dracula might arrive sooner than we think."

"Not so," said Van Helsing. "Don't forget he banqueted heavily last night, and will sleep late."

Shall I ever forget his terrible words? No!

Mina struggled hard to control her tears, but she put her hands over her face and moaned. Van Helsing was horrified at his thoughtlessness, and begged forgiveness.

"Oh, this stupid old head of mine! Please, can you forget what I said?" he asked.

"I can't forget, but there is so much in the memory that is sweet – all of you trying to help me, and rid the world of the monster, that I take it all together. Now, we must have breakfast, for we must eat in order to be strong."

Breakfast was a strange affair. We tried to be cheerful and encourage each other, and Mina, whose strength I shall always revere, was the brightest and most cheerful of all. When it was over, Van Helsing said, "We must go. We shall be back before sunset. You will be safe in our absence, Mina. I have put things in your bedroom to protect you, and to guard you against personal attack, I will touch your forehead with the crucifix."

As he did so, Mina screamed in pain. The crucifix had burned her flesh, as though it were a piece of white-hot metal. She sank to her knees, pulling her long hair over the wound, crying, "Unclean! Unclean! Even God hates my poisoned flesh!"

I held her in my arms, while our friends turned away, tears running silently down their cheeks.

"It will surely vanish," said Van Helsing, "when we rid the world of this evil, and leave your forehead as pure as the heart we know and love."

There was hope and comfort in his words. Silently, bonded by the terrible task to which we had pledged ourselves, we all knelt and prayed for help and guidance. Then we shook hands, and swore to be true to each other.

We travelled to Carfax, and entered it without trouble. Everything was the same as before. The boxes lay in the old chapel; the earth smelled musty and strong. We stood around them as Van Helsing spoke in solemn tones.

"We must sterilize this earth that Dracula has brought from a far distant land. He has chosen this spot that used to be holy. But we defeat him at his own game, for we shall make it more holy still, by sprinkling it with holy water."

One by one, we treated all the boxes. When we had finished, Van Helsing said, "So much is already done. If we are as successful elsewhere, the sunset will shine on Mina's forehead as unscarred as the day she was born."

We caught the train back into central London, and made for the house in Piccadilly, wondering how we could get into it without a key.

"I'll find a locksmith," said Arthur. "I'll pretend it's my house, and tell him I've lost my keys."

"An excellent strategy," said Van Helsing. "You have the right air of authority to make people believe you."

The ruse worked perfectly. The locksmith provided the right key and we went inside the house. Greeted by the same horrible smell as in the chapel at Carfax, we moved carefully, all keeping together in case of attack. For we did not know if the Count was hiding there.

We began our search. In the dining room we found eight boxes of earth. Only eight, not the nine we sought. Our work would not be over till we had found the last missing box. We explored the entire house, from basement to attic. No box… but we did discover evidence of Dracula's occupation. We found the title deeds of this house, as well as the houses in Mile End and Bermondsey, together with their keys. There was also a brush and comb, and a jug and basin. The basin was filled with dirty water, reddened as if by blood.

We took the keys, then destroyed the boxes, and afterward made our way to Mile End and Bermondsey to finish off the boxes there. Then we went back to Piccadilly to await the arrival of Dracula. For surely, he would come soon.

"We cannot stay here a minute after 5 o'clock," said Van Helsing. "Mina must not be left alone after sunset. We must be ready for him with a plan of attack—" Van Helsing suddenly stopped speaking and held up a warning hand. We could all hear the sound of a key being softly inserted in the lock of the hall door.

Quickly, he placed each of us in position. I was by the door, Dr. Seward by the window, and Van Helsing stood behind the door so that he could guard it while I confronted Dracula as he entered the room.

We heard slow careful steps along the hall. Dracula was evidently afraid of some surprise. Suddenly, he leapt into the room, dashing past us before we had a chance to stop him. I had a knife in my pocket, which I drew out, but I was too slow and too late. The thrust of my blade only cut the cloth of his coat. Out of it poured a stream of gold coins and a bundle of bank-notes.

Dr. Seward held up his crucifix, and I felt a mighty power fly along my body. Dracula cowered back. It is impossible to describe the expression on his face… hate, evil, rage… and bafflement. His skin was greenish-yellow, and his eyes burned red.

The next instant he grasped a handful of money from the floor, dashed across the room and threw himself at the window. Amid the crash of falling glass, he tumbled into the paved area outside. We could hear the 'ting' of some of the gold as it fell with him.

We ran over to the window and saw him spring up unhurt from the ground. He turned round and hissed up to us.

"You think you can stop me, but you will be sorry soon, each one of you. You think you have left me with no place to rest, but I have more. My revenge has only just begun. I spread it over centuries, and time is on my side. Your girls that you love are mine already, and through them, you shall be mine too. My creatures, to do what I want, whenever I want to drink."

With a contemptuous sneer, he leapt over the wall and disappeared from sight.

Van Helsing was the first to speak.

"We have learnt that, for all his brave words, he fears us, and he fears time, he fears need. If not, why the hurry? Why did he grab the money? Now we must go back to Mina, for it is late afternoon, and sunset is not far off. We must protect her. We will stay with you this night."

We found my dearest Mina waiting for us with her usual patience and cheerfulness, the hallmark of her bravery. The red scar on her forehead reminded us of her danger, while her faith against our fears, her goodness against our grim hate, in the end touched the hearts of us all.

"Jonathan," she said, "and all of you – my true friends – I know you must fight, and that you must destroy, just as you had to destroy the false Lucy. But this destruction must not be the work of hate. The poor soul, Dracula, who is the cause of all this misery, is the saddest case of all. We must think of the joy his eternal rest will give him, when he too is destroyed. You must be compassionate in your thoughts about him, too."

"If I could condemn his soul to suffer agony for all eternity," I replied, "I would rejoice."

"Oh, hush, hush, in the name of all things holy," she beseeched. "Don't say such things. I understand. These are the broken-hearted words of a very loving and sorely-tried man. But remember, whoever we are, however evil we are, all of us are in need of pity and love."

We men were all in tears, and she wept too, to know that we had listened and had been persuaded not to hate.

CHAPTER 8

THE BATTLE FOR MINA'S MIND

JONATHAN HARKER'S JOURNAL CONTINUED

OCTOBER 6

Mina and I woke before dawn. This time, we
both felt refreshed after a good night's sleep.
Turning to me, she said urgently, "Go and call Van
Helsing. I've had an idea. I want him to hypnotize
me before the sun rises, for then I shall be able to
speak freely, and tell you what Dracula is thinking.
Go quickly, dearest, for we do not have much time."

Van Helsing came hurriedly, together with
Dr. Seward.

"Hypnotism!" smiled Van Helsing. "An excellent idea. Ah, Mina, you are so brave."

Looking fixedly at her, he began the process of seeing into her mind. Mina gazed at him fixedly for a few minutes, but then gradually her eyes closed, and she sat stock still. At a certain point, when he felt he had completed these movements, Mina's eyes opened. She didn't seem to be the same woman. She had a faraway look, and her voice had a sad dreaminess. She did not appear to see us.

The stillness was broken by Van Helsing asking, "Where are you?"

"I do not know. It is all strange to me."

"What do you see?"

"Nothing. It is all dark."

"What do you hear?"

"The lapping of water. I can hear little waves leap outside."

"Then you are on a ship?"

"Oh, yes!"

"What else?"

"The sound of men running overhead. The creaking of chains…"

The voice faded away. By this time, the sun had risen and we were in full daylight. Van Helsing laid Mina down in a sleeping position, and soon she opened her eyes and stared at us in wonder.

"Have I been talking in my sleep?" she asked.

Van Helsing repeated to her what she had said, and then addressed the rest of us: "There is not a moment to lose. We now have a clue. Dracula means to escape. He saw that with only one earth-box left, London was no place for him. He has jumped on board ship… we just have to find which ship. We must ask for the list of passengers and check the cargo for Transylvania."

Dracula is out of the country! I could see the relief on Mina's face. But our task remains incomplete. We still have to trace Dracula and the missing box.

My Mina! She told me when we were alone that she had at first felt a sense of wonderful peace, as if

some haunting presence had gone from her side.
But then she caught sight of herself in the mirror,
with the red mark emblazoned on her forehead,
and she knew that she was still unclean.

Dr. Seward's Diary
October 6

We all rose early and had breakfast with a
greater air of cheerfulness than we had expected to
feel. Human nature is resilient. All of us around
the table felt the same stirrings of hope and
expectation, except for Mina. She was silent. I
could only guess why. I am sure it is because the
horrid poison of Dracula's blood has got into her,
and she cannot speak. I think her silence means
that some terrible danger lies ahead of us. She
knows, and she cannot or will not say.

After breakfast, Van Helsing called me aside.

"Have you noticed?" he whispered to me. "Mina
is changing. I can see the characteristics of the
vampire coming into her face. It is very slight, but

her teeth are sharper, and her eyes sometimes look hard. And she is silent. My fear is that just as I hypnotized her to see into Dracula's mind, so can Dracula read hers. So, my friend, I propose that we keep her ignorant of our plans, for then she cannot reveal them to him."

I nodded. "We must protect her," I said. "Jonathan will stay with her, while we go straight away to the Shipping Office, to find out which ship has already left for Transylvania."

But Mina surprised us again.

Van Helsing and I set off. We discovered that the *Czarina Catherine* had left the Thames yesterday morning. It would take her three weeks to get to Varna. We studied train timetables, and found out that we could get there ourselves, overland, in three days. But we weren't going to take any chances. Allowing for the possibilities of the ship getting there sooner than three weeks, and of our being delayed, we decided we must leave by the 17th at the latest to ensure that we arrived a few days before the ship did. We would be armed, with pistols. Just the two of us would go. Jonathan would stay behind and look after Mina.

The following morning before dawn, Mina asked us to gather around her. We have noticed that sunrise and sunset are the times of her freedom, when her old self is at liberty, without any controlling force restraining her. It comes about half an hour before sunrise and sunset, and lasts until either the sun is high, or the clouds are aglow with it setting. And then she relapses into silence.

"I know you want to go on this journey," she began, holding fast to her husband's arm. "I know you don't want me to come too. But I must. You will be safer with me, and I shall be safer too."

"But why, Mina?" asked Van Helsing. "You know that your safety is our most solemn concern. We go into danger, to which you may be more… vulnerable than any of us."

He paused, looking embarrassed.

"I know," Mina replied, pointing her finger at

her forehead. "That is why I must go. We are all here in freedom – perhaps for the last time. I can talk to you now, before the sun comes up. I may not be able to again. I know that if Dracula wills me to his side, I must obey. Trust me. I may be able to help you. You can hypnotize me, and learn from me what even I myself do not know."

We agreed. What else could we do, in the face of her courage?

"I want you to promise me," she continued, "that should the time come, you will kill me. I know I must not kill myself. I know, too, that if I were dead, you would set free my immortal soul, as you did poor Lucy's. But death is not all. I will stay alive – give up the hope of eternal rest – so long as there is a better task to be done. That is what I have to offer you. And what can you offer me in return? Your lives – not for me, but for the good of the world. Such a sacrifice is easy for brave men. But promise me, even you, my beloved husband, that when you are convinced I am so changed that I am better dead, kill me and drive a stake through my heart – and give me rest.

"And now a word of warning. It may seem, as time rolls on its relentless course, that I am in league with your enemy against you. Then you must act quickly to do what you must, so you do not lose your opportunity. Promise me, all of you, even you, my dearest husband, that you will not shrink from your duty."

We solemnly swore to do as she asked. She smiled in relief, then became even more serious.

"One last request," she said. "I want you to read the Burial Service."

She was interrupted by a deep groan from her husband as he took her hand, but she held it over her heart and continued.

"You must read it over me. You read it, my dearest, and then it will be your voice in my memory…"

"Oh my dear one," he murmured. "Death is far away from you."

"No," she said, holding up a warning finger. "I am deeper in death at this moment than if all the weight of earth from my grave lay upon me. It would comfort me to hear you read it."

She had the book ready. How can I describe that strange scene with its solemnity, its doom, its sadness, its horror? We knelt around her, with love and devotion, listening to the emotion in Jonathan's voice reading the simple and beautiful words for the Burial of the Dead. Often he said, "I – I can't – go – on –" but she was right in her instinct. Bizarre as it may seem, it comforted us all.

During the rest of that day, we prepared ourselves. We set our affairs in order, bought our tickets and, because we did not know what fate had in store for us, we made our wills.

DR. SEWARD'S DIARY, CONTINUED
OCTOBER 29
We are all in the train. This lap is from Varna to Galatz. We went from Charing Cross to Paris, and

then boarded the Orient Express. Everything should work out well. Every night, Van Helsing hypnotizes Mina to find out the progress of the *Czarina Catherine*, and we know that she is still at sea. Mina's hypnotic answer to his question, "Where are you?" is always the same. "Lapping waves, rushing water and creaking masts."

Mina seems tired and lethargic. But Van Helsing examines her teeth carefully when she is in a trance, and he says there is no sign of them sharpening. So she is in no immediate danger.

Last night her answer was different from her usual reply to Van Helsing's question.

"There are no waves lapping, we are still. I can hear men's voices calling, and the roll and creak of oars in the rowlocks. There is a tramping of feet, and ropes and chains are dragged along. There is a gleam of light. I can feel the air blowing upon me."

Here she stopped, raising her palms upwards as if lifting a weight. There was a long pause. We understood that the trance-state was passing, and with it, the time in which she could speak. Suddenly she sat up, and said in her own voice, "Would you like a cup of tea? You must all be so tired."

We said we would, wanting to please her, and she bustled off down the train to get us some.

When she had gone, Van Helsing said, "You see, my friends, Dracula is close to land. He has not yet come ashore. If he lands by day, he cannot change his shape and come ashore by himself. He needs to be carried to land in his earth-box. And if he is carried, the customs men may discover what is inside. If he lands by night, then he can change his form, and can come to shore, jumping or flying, as he must have done at Whitby. We will arrive at Galatz in the morning. We may find him in the daytime, boxed up, and at our mercy."

There was no more to be said. We waited in patience till dawn, when we might learn more from Mina's next trance.

…Mina was less able to fall so easily into her hypnotic state at dawn. I am in fear that her power of interpreting Dracula's sensations is fading. If this is so, she may ultimately mislead us. When she did speak, her words were puzzling.

"Something is leaving me. I can feel it like a cold wind. I can hear far-off, confused sounds as of men talking in a strange language, fierce-falling water, and the howling of wolves." She said no more. Van Helsing continued to question her, but she seemed to have difficulty replying. Then a minute before the sun rose, she said, "All is dark. I hear water swirling, level with my ears and the creaking of wood on wood. Cattle – I hear them, and another sound, a strange one like…"

She stopped, and grew pale.

"Go on! Speak!" said Van Helsing in an agonized voice. For even as he spoke, the sun's rays rose, reddening even Mina's pale face.

Mina opened her eyes and sat up.

"I can't remember anything," she said sweetly. "Only that I was lying here, and you said, "Go on! Speak!" as if I were a naughty child!"

The whistles are sounding. We are drawing into the station at Galatz. We are on fire with eagerness and anxiety.

JONATHAN HARKER'S JOURNAL
OCTOBER 30

When we arrived we went to find out about the *Czarina Catherine*. She was lying at anchor out in the river port. We spoke to the captain. He said that never in his life had he had such an extraordinary journey.

"It's really unusual to run from London to the Black Sea with the wind behind, as though the devil himself was blowing on our sail for his own purpose. Whenever we were near a port or headland, a fog fell on us and sailed with us, so not a thing could we see. We had to steer without being able to signal. I just let the wind carry us, for I thought if the devil wanted to get somewhere, we'd better go with him. When we got to Galatz, a man came aboard with an order written to him from

England, to receive a big box which had been put on board. I let him have it. I was uneasy about that box. If the devil had luggage aboard the ship, I'm thinking that was it."

"Where did he take it?" I asked.

"To the river, somewhere," shrugged the captain "I was glad to be rid of it."

Mina called us around her to talk. She had reached her own conclusions. She saw from the map that the river flows to the Borgo Pass. She thinks Dracula is on the river, in his box, being rowed back to his castle. She remembered hearing oars. This means that the boat is working against the current, going upstream. There would be no such noise if it were going with the flow downstream.

"We must plan what we will do," said Van Helsing.

"I shall hire a steam launch and we can follow the boat, fast," said Arthur. "We've got pistols. We can finish off that devil."

"Wait," said Van Helsing. "You two, Jonathan and Arthur, take your boat. But not me. Not Mina either. We will go to the very heart of the enemy, straight to the Castle of Dracula. Mina's hypnotic power will surely help. There is much to be done, to rid that place of evil."

I could not bear it. I blurted out, "No! You cannot take Mina into the jaws of that death trap. It is a terrible place – you hardly realize – with the very moonlight alive with horrible shapes, and every speck of dust that whirls in the wind turning into a monster." I sank down in a collapse of misery.

Mina wanted to go. She knew she could help bring this foul matter to an end. Her courage is amazing. She and Van Helsing set off in a hired horse and carriage, armed with revolvers. There may be wolves. There are snow flurries coming and going. Is this Dracula's warning?

Chapter 9

The Death of Dracula

Mina's Diary

October 31

We shall soon be off. Professor Van Helsing has got a huge bag of food for us. I have bought warm coats and rugs and shawls. We are truly in the hands of God. I don't know what will happen to us. My thoughts, as always, are of Jonathan.

November 1

All day we have journeyed, at good speed. I think the horses know they are being kindly treated, for they go willingly. The countryside is lovely, full of beauties. The people are kind, and give us hot coffee or soup if we ask for it, but they are very superstitious. When they see my scar on my forehead, they put two fingers out, as if to ward off the evil eye. They put a lot of garlic in our food, and I hate garlic. I now keep my hat and veil on, so they can't see it.

At sunset, Professor Van Helsing hypnotized me, and says that I answered as usual, "darkness, lapping water and creaking wood," so our enemy is still on the river. I am writing this in a farmhouse, where we are changing our horses. Then we shall drive through the night.

November 2

At dawn, I said in my trance, "Darkness, creaking wood and roaring water," so the river is changing as Dracula travels along it. We drove all day, seeing the countryside getting wilder. The great peaks of the Carpathian Mountains now seem to tower around us. Professor Van Helsing says we will reach the Borgo Pass in daylight. Oh, what will tomorrow bring? We will be at the place where my poor husband suffered so much.

NOTES WRITTEN BY PROFESSOR VAN HELSING
NOVEMBER 4

I am writing these notes in case I never see my friends again. It is cold, cold, and the heavy ashen sky is full of snow. I am writing this by a fire which I've kept alive all night. Mina has slept all day. She has done nothing, not even written her diary. She has lost her appetite. I tried to hypnotize her at sunset, but with no effect. The power has gone.

We got to the Borgo Pass just after sunrise yesterday morning. Mina seemed to know the road to the Castle of Dracula for, as she reminded me, it was written up by Jonathan in his journal. We went on for long hours, and Mina fell asleep. Though I tried to wake her, she slept on and on. I dared not rouse her too hard, in case I harmed her in some way. I did not like this heavy sleep for her. I was suspicious. When we met forks in the road – and it was difficult to tell if it was road, for snow had fallen thickly – I did not know which way to go. The horses seemed to have an idea, and I let them have full rein. It is now not far off sunset. The light of the dying sun falls in yellow beams over the snow, throwing long shadows on the mountains. We climb up and up and all is oh so wild and rocky, as though it were the end of the world…

I lit a fire, to make a hot supper. Mina slept still. I wrapped her in rugs, and ate, but she had nothing. She looked redder than before. I do not like it.

NOVEMBER 5

Yesterday we continued on our way, getting ever closer to the mountains. There are great precipices and wild torrents of falling water, as if nature was holding her own carnival. Mina slept all day.

At last. We had almost reached the summit of a hill, on which was a castle such as Jonathan had described. For good or ill, the end is near.

I tried to hypnotize Mina, but nothing happened. Then dark night fell around us. I fed the horses and made them some sort of shelter, and then, as I built a fire, Mina woke. I tried to make her eat, but she refused. I did eat, for I needed to be strong for what might come.

I was anxious about her. She sat by the fire, still as death, and she grew whiter and whiter, till the snow was not more pale. Not a word did she speak. But when I drew near, she clung to me, and shook with trembling from head to foot.

I drew a circle around her, and sprinkled it with holy water. There was nothing more I could do to protect her from peril.

In the night, the horses began to scream, tearing at their tethers. I quicted them, and when they felt my hands, they whinnied and licked me, and quietened down for a few minutes. Many times in the night I went to them, till, in the quietest, coldest hour of all, the fire began to die, and in the darkness I saw snow flurries and wreaths of mist coming closer... closer, and then taking shape, forming themselves into women wearing trailing garments. Was it my imagination? Had I read Jonathan's journal too closely?

The horses cowered and moaned in terror. I feared for Mina as these weird figures drew near and circled round. I stepped away from her to build up the fire, when she said, "No! Don't go outside the circle. Here you are safe."

"And you...?" I asked.

"They cannot touch me here," she said, and laughed, a low, sweet laugh.

Still I feared for her. In front of my eyes, the mist and snow materialized into three women, with bright, hard eyes, white teeth and red lips. They twined their arms and called to her in tones intolerably tender, "Come. Sister. Come to us!"

Mina's eyes were full of horror, her face twisted in repulsion. I knew, thank God, she was not yet one of them. Inside the ring, we were safe.

The horses had ceased to moan and lay still on the ground as the snow covered them. Poor beasts.

For them, there was no more terror.

At dawn, the whirling figures melted away. Mina was asleep, and I could not wake her. I will wait till the sun is high, and then enter the Castle.

NOVEMBER 5, AFTERNOON

I left Mina safely sleeping. I took a hammer with me, and broke open the castle doors, and found my way to the old chapel. The air smelled foul, making me dizzy. Far off, I heard wolves howling. I knew there were three graves to find – the graves of the vampire women.

I began to wrench away the tomb tops, till I found them lying… so beautiful they were… in their graves. Oh, it was butcher work I had to do. I hated it. But it is over! Hardly had I finished my terrible task than their bodies melted and crumbled into dust, as though death that should have come centuries ago had at last given them their peace.

There was one more tomb in the vault, more lordly than the rest. On it was one word:

DRACULA

It was empty. I sprinkled it with holy water, so he could never re-enter it. He, the Undead, would be forced to meet us elsewhere.

I returned to Mina. She was awake now, and said she knew we must go eastwards to meet Jonathan and Dr. Seward. Her lips were pale, but I was glad of that. Better than the awful redness of the vampire mouth.

MINA'S DIARY

NOVEMBER 6

I knew, somehow, that Jonathan was coming from the east. We carried our heavy wraps and stumbled downhill, looking back sometimes at the Castle in all its grandeur against the sky, standing on a precipice so high that the Carpathian Mountains seemed far below it.

A strong wind blew, making the snow swirl thickly. Between the snow flurries, though, we saw a procession of mounted men with a cart, and on the cart was a great square chest. My heart leapt as

I saw it. The evening was coming, and I knew that at sunset the thing inside would be free and could escape us. The horses were being flogged hard, and they were galloping.

"See," said Van Helsing. "They are racing for the sunset. We may be too late."

We crouched behind a rock, watching. Van Helsing had his gun ready.

Down came another rush of blinding snow, blotting out everything. When it cleared, we saw two horsemen following fast. It was Jonathan and Dr. Seward. Closer they drew, and all at once they shouted, "Stop!"

They fought their way through the crowd of men surrounding the cart with fierce purpose. At last they reached the great box, prying off the lid with their hands, using all their desperate energy. The lid began to yield. The nails gave way with a screeching sound, and the top was thrown back.

The men did not resist, but fell back. The sun had almost set. I watched its long shadows on the mountainside. I moved forward. Before me lay the terrible sight of Dracula in the box, deathly pale, his red eyes gleaming with hate. As I looked, he turned to the sinking sun, and his expression of hate turned to triumph. Then, all in an instant, I saw the sweep and flash of Jonathan's knife at his throat. It was like a miracle. Almost in the drawing of a breath, Dracula's body crumbled into dust and vanished. In the moment before he disintegrated into nothingness, there was in his face a look of peace such as I could never have imagined could rest there. I shall be glad of that as long as I live.

The Castle of Dracula now stood out against the red sky, and every stone of its broken battlements stood out against the light of the setting sun. The men who had brought the cart moved away, leaving us alone. The sun's last rays shone upon us, bathing us in a rosy glow. It must have lighted up my face, for Jonathan fell on his knees, crying, "God be thanked! The stain on her forehead has gone. She is as pure as the snow. The curse has passed away!"

It was then that I realized that this terrible ordeal really was over. The world was free of this evil, and I was released from Dracula's control, and terrible fate I feared he had condemned me to.

Post Script by Jonathan Harker

Seven years have passed since we endured these terrible things. Much and yet little has happened since. Mina and I now have a little boy. Dr. Seward is happily married. In short, we lead normal, uneventful lives. It is now almost impossible to believe the things that happened to us, and there is little proof that anything did happen, other than these letters and diaries... and who would believe these? But we have no need of proof – have no need for anyone to believe us. It is enough that we know the truth, and that one day our son will know it too.

USBORNE QUICKLINKS

Visit the Usborne Quicklinks website for links to websites where you can find out more about Bram Stoker's novel and the blood-thirsty prince, Vlad Tepes, who was the inspiration for the character Count Dracula. You can also fly over a castle in Transylvania and watch video clips of performances and movies based on the famous story of *Dracula*.

Go to www.usborne.com/quicklinks and type in the keyword 'Dracula'.

Please follow the internet safety guidelines at the Usborne Quicklinks website. Children should be supervised online.